Wonderfully Winnie!

Wilbur

Winnie the Witch

The Head Teacher

The Little Ordinaries

Wilma

Mrs Parmar

Jerry the Giant

Mr Ball

Butch/ Fluffball

The Shopkeeper

Wendy

Miss Bolshoi

OXFORD
UNIVERSITY PRESS

Great Clarendon Street, Oxford OX2 6DP

Oxford University Press is a department of the University of Oxford.
It furthers the University's objective of excellence in research, scholarship,
and education by publishing worldwide in

Oxford   New York

Auckland   Cape Town   Dar es Salaam   Hong Kong   Karachi
Kuala Lumpur   Madrid   Melbourne   Mexico City   Nairobi
New Delhi   Shanghai   Taipei   Toronto

With offices in
Argentina   Austria   Brazil   Chile   Czech Republic   France   Greece
Guatemala   Hungary   Italy   Japan   Poland   Portugal   Singapore
South Korea   Switzerland   Thailand   Turkey   Ukraine   Vietnam

Oxford is a registered trade mark of Oxford University Press
in the UK and in certain other countries

Nitty Winnie first published in 2012
Spooky Winnie first published in 2013
Winnie Goes Wild! first published in 2013
This edition first published in 2015

British Library Cataloguing in Publication Data:
Data available

ISBN: 978-0-19-273928-5 (paperback)

2 4 6 8 10 9 7 5 3 1

Printed in Great Britain

Paper used in the production of this book is a natural, recyclable product made
from wood grown in sustainable forests. The manufacturing process conforms
to the environmental regulations of the country of origin

Laura Owen and Korky Paul

Wonderfully Winnie!

OXFORD
UNIVERSITY PRESS

Contents

Winnie's Wet Weekend

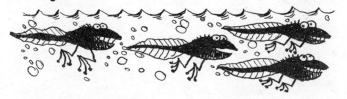

Plip! Plop! Water drip-dropped down
from Winnie's ceiling. **Slosh!** Winnie's
wellies waded ankle-deep through the
water and **slap-splash!** her broom-
mop squelched water into a bucket.

'Oh, soggy blooming sausages!' moaned
Winnie. 'We'll have to start building an ark
soon, Wilbur!'

'Mrrow,' agreed Wilbur, shivering on a
high-up shelf.

'I hope Jerry can mend our leak soon,' said Winnie. 'Or we'll all get flushed out of the house just like . . .'

Wallop!-clonggggg! went Jerry's mallet on the water tank upstairs, and moments later—sloossh!—water came pouring, tumbling down the staircase. It was now up to Winnie's knobbly knees.

Croak! said a happy frog who was gazing up at Winnie. Splish-splosh danced tadpoles like mini dolphins. Swish-slither swam an eel towards Winnie.

'Eeek!' Winnie scrambled up to join Wilbur on the shelf. **Creak!** went the shelf because it wasn't built for the weight of witches. 'Well, that's it!' said Winnie, as the shelf tipped them both—**splash!**—into the flood. 'If I'm going to wade in water and shrivel my toes to raisin-wrinkles, I'd rather wade and shrivel in warm water and in the sunshine.

Maybe even licking a nice-cream! Let's go
to the seaside!'

'Meeow!' agreed Wilbur. He didn't
much like the wet sea, but he did like
sunshine and nice-creams.

So Winnie waved her wand.
'Abracadabra!'

And instantly they were at the seaside.

'Ah!' sighed Winnie, kicking off her wellies and tucking her dress into her knickers. 'Just look at that sea sparkling like a beetle's back!'

'Mrrow,' scowled Wilbur.

'You're right,' said Winnie. 'I've had enough wetness for today, too. Let's make a sandcastle instead.'

They dug a moat and threw all the
sand into the middle to make a big castle
mound. Then they shovelled sand into
Winnie's hat, and upended it to make
turrets. They used Winnie's wand to
scrape door and window shapes, and they
slapped on shells to make it all look lovely.

'There! As pretty as a ferret in fairy wings!' said Winnie. 'I reckon we've earned ourselves a lice-lolly!'

They couldn't decide which flavour lice-lollies to choose, so they had four each ... which meant a lot of fast licking— **slurp slurp!**—and sticky paws. Then they used the lolly sticks to make a drawbridge over the moat.

'Ah!' sighed Winnie. 'I'd love to be a princess living in our castle instead of a witch living in a flooded house. D'you know, Wilbur, I think . . .' Winnie picked up her wand.

'Meeeow!' Wilbur leapt to grab the wand from Winnie's hand to stop her from waving it. But he was too late.

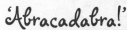

'Abracadabra!'

17

Winnie was a princess. A very very tiny princess, just the right size to fit into their sandcastle.

'Mrrrow!' said Wilbur, trying to catch her as if she was a mouse. But tiny Princess Winnie had picked up her skirts and run over the drawbridge and into the castle before he could stop her.

18

'Oh!' said Winnie as she looked around. 'Oh, how princessy!'

There were seashell dishes and cups on a table sculpted in the sand. There were seaweed hammocks swinging in the breeze outside. There was a crab neighing in the sand-stable. Winnie flung herself into the saddle. 'Giddy-up!' she said.

But—**swerve-whoops!** the crab
scuttled sideways. 'Eeeeeeerrrrrr,' said
Winnie, holding on tight. 'Please stop!'
Plop! Off she fell, then she staggered, all
dizzy-dizzy, before, 'Eeeek!' she screamed
because there was a huge eye looking
through the sand-stable door at her.

'Meeeow!' Wilbur was trying to tell her
something urgent.

'What water?' Winnie leaned out of the
stable door.

Slop! A wave whacked against the wall
of the castle, saltily slapping Winnie in the
face.

'Heck in a handkerchief, the blooming
tide's coming in!' said Winnie. 'And it's
crumbling my walls!'

Wilbur dug, trying to make the moat take water around the castle instead of through it. But the sea is big and powerful, and Winnie's princess castle was small and made of sand.

'Help!' shouted Winnie. 'This castle is collapsing!' The wet walls were sagging and slipping all around her. 'Where's my wand?' wailed Winnie.

22

But she'd left it out on the sand.

'It'll get washed away! And I'm sinking into the sand! It's sucking me in as if I was a string of spaghetti in a monster's mouth. Oh, Wilbur!'

Wilbur was dig-dig-digging so fast his paws and spade were a blur. But the tide was rising higher and higher, and the castle was crumbling lower and lower. What could Winnie do? Then she saw the lolly stick drawbridge, bobbing on top of the water. 'A raft!' shouted tiny Winnie.

23

And she heaved herself up onto it in a very un-princesslike way. Suddenly— *slurp!*—a wave sploshed the raft and Winnie out to sea.

'Wilburrrrrr!' shouted Winnie as the raft bucked like a bronco under her. Wilbur pounced. He batted the raft with his paw and sent it—*plop!*—to land on the sand.

Up jumped Winnie. She grabbed her wand. It was huge for her now. But Winnie heaved the wand as if she was a Scotsman tossing the caber, and—**tip-crash!**—it waved as it fell, and Winnie shouted, '*Abracadabra!*'

And there she was, full-sized, again.

'Thank knitted noodles for that!' said
Winnie. The sandcastle was just a sad little
hump in the sand under the water now.
'Let's go home. At least there are no tides
at home,' said Winnie.

They flew home to see Winnie's house looking beautiful. The dark clouds and rain had cleared. The sun had come out. There was a rainbow in the sky.

'Just like when Noah's flood was at an end,' said Winnie. 'Oh, I do hope that our flood has gone too.'

The house was still damp. It had squelch-soggy carpets and murky marks on the walls. But the water had gone. Winnie yawned. 'You know, Wilbur, I don't fancy a bath tonight somehow.' She went to clean her teeth . . . and there was the same frog, sitting and looking at Winnie lovingly and pouting his lips.

'Hmm,' pondered Winnie. 'You know what, Wilbur? When princesses kiss frogs they turn into handsome princes. D'you suppose that since I was a princess today it might work for me?'

28

She was just reaching out a hand to let the frog step onto it when—*pow!*— Wilbur's paw batted the frog right out of the window.

'Oh, Wilbur! Now I'll never know!'

'Meeow,' agreed Wilbur, and he settled himself onto Winnie's bed.

Jurassic Winnie

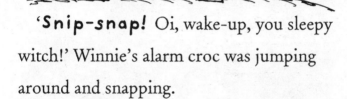

'**Snip-snap!** Oi, wake-up, you sleepy witch!' Winnie's alarm croc was jumping around and snapping.

'What do you want, you naggy croc?' asked Winnie's sleepy slow voice from under the bed covers.

'Get up, get up, get up! **Snip-snap!** You're late!'

'Late?' Winnie sat up and looked at the croc. 'Late for what? Oh pickled

porcupines, in just thirteen minutes
I'm meant to be at the little ordinaries'
swap shop!'

Winnie tugged off her nightie, and
tugged on her clothes so fast she looked
like the contents of a tumble dryer. She
hadn't got time to brush her hair. The
alarm croc tapped his foot and tutted.

'I know! I know!' wailed Winnie. 'I'm going as fast as I blooming well can!' She slid down the stairs to save some time. Then she ran into the kitchen where she poured sneereal into a bowl.

'Meeow?' complained Wilbur, his tummy rumbling.

'All right, all right!' said Winnie as she
tried to put catfish biscuits into a bowl for
him at the same time as putting ditchwater
into the kettle, but ended up pouring
ditchwater onto Wilbur's head and biscuits
into the teapot. She put a spoonful of
sneereal into her mouth.

Pah—spit! 'Yucky-mucky-duckies, why ever would somebody put a . . .' Winnie looked at the soggy card she'd picked from her teeth, '. . . a picture of a brontosaurus in a packet of sneereal?' Winnie threw the card into the bin.

Just then, **Boom boom! Cuckoo! Snip-snap! Brrr!** All the clocks in Winnie's house went off at once.

'Flying fish fingers, we've run out of time! Off to the swap shop! I've got a lovely jigsaw with only three bits missing that I want to swap for something nice.'

In the school hall the children were busy swapping, but they were only swapping cards.

'Jurassic World cards,' explained one of the children. 'If you collect the whole set you get given a book about the dinosaurs who lived then.'

'That's wonderful!' said Winnie. 'Oo, where do I get the cards from? I want one of those books. I think some of my ancestors might have been Jurassic.'

'The cards come in packets of Snip Crockle and Poop cereal,' said a child.

'Meeow!' pointed out Wilbur.

'Oh!' said Winnie. 'Do you think that brontosaurus thingy was one of them?'

'The BRONTOSAURUS?' shouted the children. 'That's the card we all need! It's the only card left to find, and nobody's got one. You have to have a complete set by tomorrow to get the book!'

'Oh dilly-doodles!' said Winnie.

'If you give your brontosaurus card to me, I'll give you a velociraptor,' said a boy.

'I'll give you two triceratops!' shouted a girl.

'I'll give you . . . !' shouted all the children at once.

'Heck in a hole, I'd better go and find that blooming card I half ate,' said Winnie.

Winnie rushed home and threw
everything out of the bin, looking for what
was left of the brontosaurus card. But—
eeek!—a rat was just nibbling at the last
corner of the card, chewing the very tip of
the brontosaurus tail.

'Too late!' said Winnie. 'Those little
ordinaries aren't going to be pleased.

Oh, if only I could go back in time and do this morning all over again. Then I'd look after that card. Oo, I know! I'll magic myself to go back in time!'

'Meeow!' warned Wilbur. But Winnie did the most enormous sweep of her wand. *Abracadabra!'*

Time whirled back hundreds of millions of years in a blur, and it dropped Winnie and Wilbur in a strange hot wilderness of plants and insects and smells. 'Er . . . this is a bit further back in time than I had in mind,' said Winnie. 'This might be actual Jurassic times.' Winnie looked around. **Scrunch-munch!**—she heard a noise.

'Hiss!' went Wilbur, the fur on his back sticking up like a toothbrush.

'What is THAT?' said Winnie.

Scrunch-munch! 'Oooooo!' **Thump-bump!** 'Er ... um ... uh-oh!' Winnie was looking up at something the size and shape of a lighthouse that had just whumphed down in front of her.

'M-m-meeow!' said Wilbur, as he pointed a claw up and up and up and ...

'Oh, my wormy-woolly-word!'
said Winnie, backing away. Towering
over Winnie and Wilbur was the most
enormous brontosaurus! Down came its
great big head on a long long neck the
length and thickness of a fat tree trunk.
Sniff! went the brontosaurus.

'Er . . . nice Bronty!' said Winnie in a
wobbly voice. She tickled its chin. 'Who's
a very big boy, then? Can I take your
photo, please?' Winnie whipped out her
mobile moan that also worked as a camera.
'Say "cheese!"' said Winnie, stepping back
and back and back to try and get the whole
of the huge dinosaur into her photograph.

'Squeak!' said the brontosaurus just
as Winnie was about to click, making it a
very shaky shot.

45

'Oh, bother! Please, Mr Brontosaurus, could we just try that one more time?' asked Winnie. 'Thanks ever so. Say "silly sausages!" Mr B!'

'Tweet-tweet!' said the brontosaurus.

Click!

CLICK!

'Ooer, look what saw us!' Winnie pointed to a whole group of dinosaurs who'd gathered to pose for their photos to be taken too. A triceratops, a diplodocus, some little dinomice, and a great big velociraptor. And then . . .

Crash! Grrr! Rooaarrr!

Winnie looked over her shoulder.

'Oooer! I spy with my little eye

something beginning with 'T'—a great

big tyrannosaurus rex! Quick, Wilbur!'

Winnie waved her wand. *Abracadabra!'*

Whooosh! And they were home.

Winnie printed out the photos, making lots of the brontosaurus one.

'Copies for each of the little ordinaries,' said Winnie. 'Then they can all get the Jurassic book.'

Back at the school, 'Yay, now we've got complete sets!' shouted the children when Winnie gave them the photos.

But, 'Ahem, I think not!' said the Snip Crockle and Poop cereal man. 'These aren't the official pictures.'

'They're better than pictures; they're photographs!' said Winnie.

'Do you think I'm stupid?' said the man. 'Who ever heard of a brontosaurus being pink?'

'But they ARE!' said Winnie.

'Nonsense!' said the cereal man. 'There'll be no Jurassic World book for any of you!'

51

'Oh, Winnie!' shouted the children.

'Huh! The books are as rubbish as a very smelly rubbish dumpy tip anyway,' said Winnie. 'They've got lots of stuff wrong in them. Did you know that a T-rex is bright blue?'

'Really?' said the children.

'Yep. And that a brontosaurus goes tweet-tweet!' said Winnie. 'And . . .'

Winnie and Wilbur had a happy afternoon telling and showing the children some real things about dinosaurs that the people who write books hadn't yet discovered.

The cereal man went home. He looked
at the photo of the brontosaurus. Beside
the brontosaurus was a witch-shaped
shadow.

The cereal man sat and he wondered . . .

54

A Wedding for Winnie

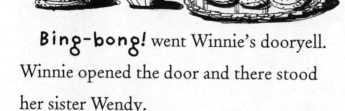

Bing-bong! went Winnie's dooryell. Winnie opened the door and there stood her sister Wendy.

Sniff! went Wendy. **Sob!**

'Oh dear!' said Winnie. 'Your eyes are leaking! Here, have a hankie-pankie. Come in and have some nice ditchwater tea and a toasted scrumpet.'

Sigh! Sniff! Sob! went Wendy.

'Oh, Winnie, I get so lonesome, all on my

ownsome. Can I come and live with you?'

'Er . . .' said Winnie, who really didn't want a weeping Wendy living with her. 'You should get a cat, Wendy. Wilbur's both friend and hot water bottle to me.'

'Meeow!' said Wilbur, carrying in a tray of hot spluttered scrumpets.

'Oh dear!' said Wendy. 'A-a-a-atishoo! Cats make me sneeze! Go away, Wilbur!'

'Mrrow!' Out stomped cross Wilbur.

'Get a dog, then,' said Winnie. 'Or a kangaroo, or a baboon.'

'No!' wailed Wendy. 'Anything furry makes me sneeze.'

'A snake?' said Winnie.

But Wendy shuddered at the thought.

Then she smiled. 'A man might be cuddly!'

'Oo, I've heard that men are more
trouble than cats and dogs,' said Winnie.
'And they have hair.'

'But a man would be romantic!' said
Wendy.

'Well, there's Mr Ball at the garage.
D'you think you could make a catch
out of him? Shall I send him a message?'

'Yes please!' said Wendy.

So, *Abracadabra!* Winnie waved her wand. And down flew a pink lovey-dove with a reply note in its beak.

♥ ·MR BALL· ♥
would be delighted
to meet a beautiful
LADY
WITH A VIEW TO POSSIBLE
♥ MARRIAGE ♥

Sigh! 'I feel less lonely already!' said Wendy.

59

Lovey-doves flapped back and forth, dropping and collecting notes as fast as Wendy could read and write them. Wendy got pinker with every note she read. And then came one that made her bright red.

'Ooer, he wants me to marry him!' said Wendy in a wobbly voice.

'Don't you want to meet him before you say "yes"?' said Winnie. 'I wouldn't even buy a toenail clipper without taking a look at it first.'

'But I love him!' said Wendy. **Sigh!** 'Oh, I want a very special wedding. And I want you to be my bridesmaid, Winnie!'

'Me?' said Winnie. She'd gone as red as a boiled bog-berry. 'Really truly?'

Winnie glanced through the window at a scowling Wilbur and did the thumbs-up. If she could get Wendy married, then soon Wilbur could come inside. 'Oh, Wendy, I'll make it a really really special wedding,' said Winnie. 'Just tell me what you want!'

Wendy did. She lay on the sofa and leafed through wedding magazines showing flowery, flouncy, fantastic weddings.

NEEE OOW!

And Winnie set off like a burst balloon
—**neeeoow!**—to get all the things that
Wendy wanted as fast as possible.

'I want lots and lots of smelly-welly
flowers!' **Sigh!** said Wendy.

'Stinkwort and pongberry and wiffle-
lillies,' said Winnie. **Neeeoow!**

Off she went into the garden to snip and collect smelly flowers and thistles and dandelions. Wilbur was sulking too much to help. **Neeeoow!** Back into the house went Winnie.

'I want a beautiful fruitiful wedding cake with thirteen layers, and pink icing all over it!' said Wendy.

'Heck in a hiccupping hippopotamus!' said Winnie. But—**neeeoow!**—she did her best—**stir slop slap splatter!**

'I can cook better when I've got Wilbur helping,' said Winnie sadly.

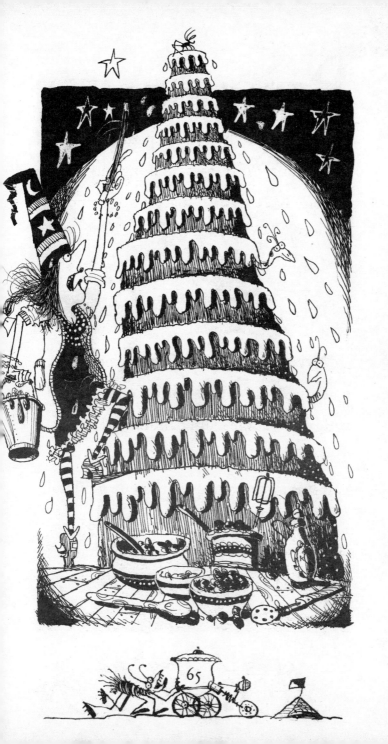

'Never mind about Wilbur. I want balloons!' said Wendy. So Winnie chewed and blew bubble-gum balloons, getting herself in a sticky-poppy mess.

'I want a dress like a meringue mountain with a long long train,' said Wendy.

So—*neeeoow!*—Winnie did her best with a bed sheet and magic.

Abracadabra!

'And I want a Hen Party!' said Wendy.

'What in the wobbly world is one of those?' asked Winnie.

'I don't know, but I want one,' said Wendy.

So Winnie waved her wand.

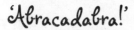'Abracadabra!'

Instantly the room was full of hens, all flapping and pecking and cluck-cluck-squawking! They pecked the balloons—**pop!**—and laid eggs and dropped droppings and . . .

'Oh, if only Wilbur was here to herd them into order!' said Winnie. 'Quick!' she told Wendy. 'Get into the dress and get married before anything else goes wrong!'

Neeeeow! Winnie zipped and glued and pinned and buttoned and stitched Wendy into her dress, then she coupled the train onto the back of it. Then— **neeeoow!**—Winnie did her best with a teasel brush and cockroach hairclips to make Wendy's hair nice.

'There,' said Winnie, standing still at last. 'You look as lovely as a little lamb licking a lolly.'

'I want a veil, too!' said Wendy.

'Really?' said Winnie who was too tired to **neeeow!** any more. So she just reached out for some cobwebs, and draped them, spiders and all, over Wendy's head.

'There!' said Winnie. 'You're done.'

'But you're not!' wailed Wendy. 'And really I did want two bridesmaids!'

That gave Winnie an idea. 'You go, and I'll follow in a mini-moment,' said Winnie. 'Wilbur!' she called at the door. 'Come here, Wilbur!'

Swish!—she waved her wand. *'Abracadabra!'* She magicked a flouncy-bouncy dress with hooped underskirts. **Swish!**—*'Abracadabra!'* She magicked another cat-sized one.

'Mrrow!' said Wilbur in disgust.

'Oh, pleeease be a bridesmaid with me!'
said Winnie. 'I've been missing you so
much!' So Wilbur let himself be buttoned
and ribboned. 'Just hold those flowers
right in front of your face,' said Winnie.
'Nobody will guess that you're not a little
twirly girly!'

The wedding was very special, just as
Winnie had promised. Mr Ball looked a bit
nervous about marrying somebody that
he couldn't see beneath the cobweb veil.
But Winnie had forgotten exactly why
Wendy had said that she couldn't be near
to Wilbur. As the short furry bridesmaid
with a tail sticking out came up behind the
bride and bridegroom . . .

73

'**A-h-ah-tishoo!**' sneezed Wendy, and **whoops!** the veil blew right off her face, showering thistle and dandelion seeds all around her.

'Ah!' sighed Mr Ball.

'Phewy-dewy-dumplings!' whispered Winnie. 'He likes her!'

Mr Ball and Wendy liked each other so much they didn't really notice much about the wedding except each other . . . which was just as well, really!

As the new Mrs Ball and her husband flew off on her broom into the sunset, Winnie hugged Wilbur tight.

'A man might be more romantic, Wilbur, but I'm glad that I share my life with you!'

'Purrrrr!' said Wilbur proudly. He had forgotten quite how silly he was looking.

76

Nitty Winnie

La-di-tiddly-doo-daa!

'What's that music?' said Winnie.
'Ooo, look! The little ordinaries are
dancing around a pole that's as stripy
as my socks, and they've all got ribbons!'

Red, blue, orange, yellow, and green
ribbons were twiddling and weaving
together in a beautiful pattern as the
children skipped around and under
each other.

'Oh, that's as lovely as a baby newt in a nettle flower bonnet!' said Winnie. 'Ooo, please, Mrs Parmar, can I join in?'

'I don't think that's a very good . . .' began Mrs Parmar.

But, 'Oh yes, please DO join in!' said a bubbly dance teacher. 'The more the merrier, I say!'

'Brillaramaroodles!' said Winnie. She grabbed a yellow ribbon and plunged into the dance, skipping as high as a kangaroo jumps.

Tiddily jump-bump!

'Hey!'

Diddily slip-trip!

'Ow!'

Winnie wasn't weaving in and out of the children, and nor was she weaving her ribbon in with the other ribbons. She was crashing and tripping and going in the wrong direction to make such a tangle of ribbons that it all looked like multi-coloured spaghetti.

'Oo heck, what a lot of knots!' said Winnie as the music stopped.

'WINNIE!' shouted Mrs Parmar. 'That is NOT how it should be done!'

'No. No, it really isn't,' agreed Miss Bolshoi the dance teacher who had wilted like a dejected daffodil and didn't look nearly as bubbly as before.

'Oh, I'm ever so sorry, Mrs P,' said
Winnie. She looked at the children tangled
with the ribbons. 'Heck in a haddock!'
she said. 'That doesn't look good, does it.
Don't you worry, though. I'll soon sort it!'

'Oh, please . . .' began Mrs Parmar, but
Winnie was already waving her wand.

'Abracadabra!'

And instantly the ribbons came to life,
like skinny bright eels, untangling knots
and then swishing this way and that and
tying the children and Winnie firmly
to the pole. They were soon bound and
gagged by ribbons woven into a tight
criss-cross pattern.

'Mmmnff,' said Winnie, who had purple
ribbon over her mouth.

'A sturdy pair of scissors is the only cure,' said Mrs Parmar. 'And—**snip snip!**—she cut the children and Winnie free.

'That's better!' said Winnie. 'I'd got an itch on my head and no hands able to reach up and scratch it.' **Scrabbly-scratch!** She gave her head a good old scratch now. 'Aah, that's better!'

'But the ribbons are ruined!' wailed Mrs Parmar. 'We can't possibly do any more dancing now. You must all go home for lunch, and I shall have to see if I can buy more ribbons.'

'Dear, oh dear, oh dear,' said Miss Bolshoi. 'And people are coming to watch us this afternoon. Oh dear.'

'Come back at four o'clock sharp,' Mrs Parmar told the children. 'All neat and clean and wearing your best dress if you're a girl and best bow tie if you're a boy. We mustn't let the public down. Oh, I do hope that I can get hold of more ribbons!'

'I'll be there, smart and neat, Mrs P,' promised Winnie.

'Oh dear,' said Miss Bolshoi and Mrs Parmar together.

Winnie and Wilbur went home. **Itch itch** went Winnie's head.

'Hardboiled hiccups!' said Winnie, scratching at her hair. 'What in the whoopsy world is it that's making me so itchy?'

'Meeow?' Wilbur peered and poked at Winnie's hair. 'Mrrrow!' He held up something teeny-tiny and black.

'Whatever is that?' said Winnie.

Wilbur put the teeny-tiny black thing on a bit of white paper. He handed Winnie a magnifying glass.

'It's a lousy louse!' said Winnie. 'Oh, no, I've got nits! Flipping frog flippers,

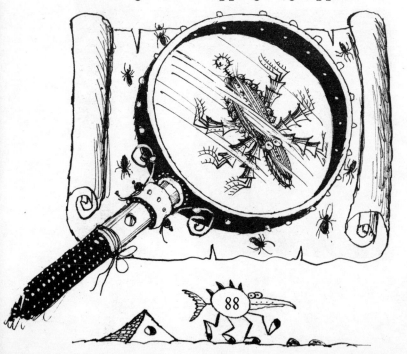

I'm infested! I must have caught them off those little ordinaries when we were tied tight together!' **Scritch-scratch!** Winnie was scrubbing at her head and dancing around. Wilbur took a step or two back.

'Mrrow!'

'Don't worry, cats don't get lice,' said Winnie.

Scratch-scritch! 'Oo, I can't stand this, Wilbur. I must catch them all . . . and then we can sprinkle them on our frogspawn rice pudding for lunch. They may be nice to eat, but they're horrible to be a home to!'

Winnie looked in the mirror, pulling her nasty nest of knotted nitty hair about so that she could try and see what was lurking inside it.

'It's no blooming good,' she said. 'The little lice are black, the same as my hair, so I just can't see them. Oo, I know!' She grabbed her wand. *'Abracadabra!'*

91

Instantly Winnie's hair was green.

'Now we can see them!' said Winnie. 'Little black crawly-creepy itch. 'Oo, there's one!' **Snatch!** 'And another!' **Pinch!** 'Can you do the ones round the back of my head, Wilbur?'

It wasn't easy, searching through the tangle of hair, and the searching made the tangles worse.

'It's not exactly neat and smart in the way Mrs P wanted, is it?' said Winnie, prodding her mess of hair. 'I'd better get a better hairdo before we go back to the dancing. *Abracadabra!*'

But none of the styles Winnie tried
looked right, until, *Abracadabra!* ...

93

Oo, I like that one! Don't you, Wilbur?
Now, there's just time to get into my
dancing dress, then off we go. I'm sure
Mrs Parmar and Miss Bolshoi will be
very happy to see me.'

Winnie was delighted to be greeted warmly. Wilbur was surprised.

'Oh, welcome, welcome!' said Miss Bolshoi. 'You are just what we need!'

'Really?' said Winnie. 'I *knew* I was a good dancer after all!'

'Dancer? No, no, I don't want you to dance at all. You have a very important part to play in our ribbon dancing, but not as a dancer.'

'Then you mean . . .' began Winnie as she was hustled into the centre of things and the children all surged towards her.

'Remember, take hold of one ribbon each!' trilled Miss Bolshoi. 'Are you ready?' She pushed a button, and the music started.

La-di-tiddly-doo-daa!

And there was Winnie, as tall and stripy as a pole, with ribbons dangling from the top of her head, and the children dancing round and round.

'Oooer!' said Winnie, getting dizzy. She blinked and concentrated hard, and managed not to fall over.

'Oo, well I am quite good at this sort of dancing,' she said.

She was. And when the dance was over, Winnie looked like this.

Winnie's Time Machine

Winnie looked at her garden, and sighed.
'That flower bed looks like a noodle-
doodle salad with added slugs on the side.
Still, it'll look better when I've planted this
nice lolly-lily plant. And it'll give me fresh
lollies to pick all summer long! Now, what
can I find for the lolly-lily plant to grow
up?'

Winnie stuck her spade into the earth,
and was about to dig when,

Crash! Ting! Ping!
'Oh dear, oh no, oh blow!'

'That's Jerry next door,' said Winnie to Wilbur. 'Come on, catman, let's see what he's up to.'

High over the fence leapt Winnie the Witch, and Wilbur scrabbled over after her. They opened Jerry's giant front door,

and—*sploosh!*—out swept Scruff the
dog, surfing a frothy warm wave of water.

'What in the witchy world?' began
Winnie.

'It's me washing machine,
Missus,' said Jerry, squelching through
a soggy pile of clothes. 'I was just
washing me smalls when me
machine started banging.

101

I couldn't find me hammer, so
I gave it a tap with me mallet
instead and, well . . . it's broke!
I've got nuffink to wear now!'

'I'll do your washing in my machine if
you like,' said Winnie. Wilbur put his head
in his paws, but,

'Oh, fanks, Missus!' said Jerry.

Winnie had forgotten that Jerry's smalls
weren't small at all. Jerry's smalls were huge!

'It only takes three of his great soggy pongy socks to completely fill my little machine,' said Winnie. **Squirt-slosh-churn-rattle-sigh-clunk!** went her washing machine as it worked on the giant socks. 'How am I going to fit all his other clothes into it?' she wondered.

Then Winnie pulled out something from a pocket in Jerry's huge overalls. 'It's Jerry's hammer! No wonder his machine was banging!'

Worse than doing all the washing was hanging it up to dry. Wilbur helped Winnie to heave a giant shirt the size of a sofa cover onto her washing line. The sleeves trailed into the dirt because it was so big, and then—

TWANG!

—the washing line collapsed under the
weight.

'Jitterbug juice jelly, the whole
blooming lot is dirty again!' said Winnie.
'Jerry!' she shrieked. 'You'll have to put up
a new washing line for us!'

Jerry tied a washing line between two tree tops, then Winnie and Wilbur flew up on the broom to peg his pants and socks and hankies and shirts.

106

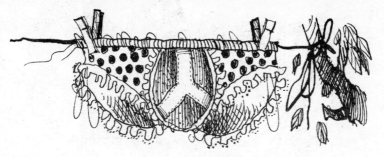

'I never knew you wore such fancy pants!' said Winnie, and Wilbur snickered behind a paw as Jerry blushed as red as a squashed tomato. 'There!' said Winnie, standing back to admire her work. 'All done!'

Flash! Thunder! Rumble!

'Oh, no!' said Winnie. 'Please don't rain!' But it did rain, very hard.

'How's the washing going to get dry now?' said Winnie. 'Poor Jerry's shivering with cold. He needs some clothes, and none of my clothes would fit him, even if he did want to borrow a purple dress.'

107

Winnie shook rain from her hair.
'Honestly!' said Winnie. 'I've got a
machine to wash clothes, a machine to
toast toadstool crumpets, machines for just
about everything. But what I really need
now is a machine to . . .' She was about
to say, 'dry the washing', when Wilbur
pointed at the clock.

'Meow!' he said. It was time for his
favourite *Mice in the Attic* television
programme. But the clock made Winnie
think of something else.

'Wilbur, you're a genius!' she said.
'That's it! We'll make a machine to turn
the time back to *before* Jerry broke his
washing machine. Then everything will be
hunky-snory!'

108

They gathered chairs and levers and
knobs and buttons, and the clock, of
course.

'Stand back!' said Winnie, waving her
wand, *Abracadabra!*

CLATTER-CLUNK-CLUNK!

'Behold a monstrously magnificent marvellous time machine!' announced Winnie. They put on cauldron smash helmets and climbed into the machine.

110

'Right,' said Winnie. 'Set it for eight o'clock this morning.' Wilbur was just setting the clock when . . .

A flash of lightning made them all jump and Wilbur's clock-setting went a bit haywire.

ZOOM! SHAKE! RATTLE AND ROLL!

They were speeding through time and space.

III

'W-w-w-where, or w-w-w-when, are we going to, I w-w-w-wonder?' said Winnie, clutching on tight.

'D-d-d-dunno, Missus!' said Jerry.

Bump! They landed in a damp dark cave.

'Ooer-er-er!' said Winnie, her voice echoing. 'Wherever are we-we-we?'

'Meow!' Wilbur pointed to where a fire was burning at the cave entrance. 'Goodee-ee-ee,' said Winnie and her echo. 'There must be somebody here-ere-ere-ere.'

But they couldn't see anybody. Just a drawing on the cave wall.

'Whoever lives here has a cat,' said Winnie. 'And a dog. So they must be ever so friendly!'

'They's got giant h'animals!' said Jerry, picking up some huge bones.

Gulp! went Wilbur, pointing a claw at something, or somebody, in the cave opening.

'Er, I fink it might be time to go, Missus,' said Jerry because the person at the cave entrance didn't look ever so friendly after all. She was holding a spear!

114

'Oggle-bog-flog!' shouted the cave
woman, just as the ground started to shake
and a huge hairy mammoth went running
by with a whole lot of men and funny-
looking cats chasing after it.

'Er, time to go home, and quick!' said
Winnie. 'Hold tight!' Winnie waved her
wand, 'Abracadabra!'

Whirl-swirl-twirl-clatter.

They landed back in Winnie's kitchen with the rain still splattering the windows.

'Safe and sound!' said Winnie. 'But what was all that clattering?'

'It was them bones,' said Jerry. 'They came back wiv me.'

'Hmm, I wonder what kind of critter they belonged to?' said Winnie. 'Let's see.' Winnie waved her wand, **'Abracadabra!'**

And the bones came together in a rather odd-looking way.

'Oh! I don't think five legs and two tails can be right, can it?' said Winnie.

She waved her wand again. '*Abracadabra!*'

'That's not right either.'

Another wave. '*Abracadabra!* Ooh, it's a mega-mammoth skellington!' said Winnie.

A mammoth skeleton made the perfect clothes rack for drying giant-sized clothes.

After all that adventure, Winnie planted
her lolly-lily, and it turned out that a
mammoth skeleton is just what you need
for a lolly-lily plant to grow up.

Winnie the Shadowitch

One dark evening, Winnie clicked the switch to turn on her lights, but everything stayed dark.

'The power's gone off!' said Winnie. 'We'll have to use Wee Willie Winkie candles until it's on again.'

Winnie and Wilbur weren't sure what they ate for supper. They could hardly see what they were cooking or eating in the flickering candlelight.

'Well, that meal was a culinary mystery tour,' said Winnie, picking bits from between her teeth. 'Now, what shall we do with our evening, Wilbur?' They couldn't watch telly or see well enough to read. But Winnie had another way to share a story with Wilbur. 'I know, I'll tell you a ghost story,' she said.

Wilbur got ready to listen.

'Once upon a time,' began Winnie.
She lifted her arms dramatically, and her
shadow on the wall suddenly became a
huge pouncing shape. Wilbur's fur went
up on end. On went Winnie. 'Once upon
a time there was a big dark house full of
creaks and groans and spiders and rats.

Just like this house, really.' Winnie leant over, and made her voice whispery. 'But the story house was in a wild wood full of whooshy wind and wailing bats. It was as dark as liquorice leeches.'

Wilbur shivered, eyes as big as mushrooms.

'And in this house a cat lived all on his little-old owny-oh,' said Winnie. 'That cat was called Tiddles.'

Wilbur rolled his eyes, but Winnie carried on.

'One dark day, Tiddles heard a **scratch-scritch-scratch.** Just the mice under the floor, thought Tiddles.

But the sound came again. **Scratch-scritch-scratch.** And it wasn't coming from under the floor now. It was coming from above his head. It must be rats in the roof, thought Tiddles. But then the scratching came again, right behind him and louder than ever. **Scratch-scritch-scratch.** Tiddles felt a tap on his shoulder, and he turned and saw . . .'

'**Hiss!**' went Wilbur.

'. . . a ghost! And the ghost said, "So sorry to disturb you, Tiddles my old fruit bat, but I've got this terrible itch in the middle of my back, and I just can't reach the spot however much I scratch. Will you scratch it for me?"'

'Meow!' said Wilbur.

127

'You're right,' said Winnie. 'It was a silly story. Bedtime now. Up we go.'

But the staircase was dark and dithery in the candlelight.

'Oo, this is spooky!' said Winnie, as she felt her way onto the first step. Her candlelight lurched around the family portraits all the way up. Their eyes seemed to follow her and their mouths seemed to leer and cackle. 'Horrible, aren't they,' whispered Winnie.

By the time they got to the top of the stairs, Winnie's and Wilbur's knees were knocking like a pocket full of eyeball marbles. As they hurried to bed, Winnie said, 'Let's paint some nice new portraits in the morning, and put them up the stairs instead. Nice pictures of us and our friends.'

'Purr!' agreed Wilbur.

So, next morning, Winnie got out paints
and paper and easels and overalls, and she
took them all outside into the sunshine.
'You paint me, and I'll paint you,' she told
Wilbur.

Splash-splat-whoops-splot!

'Er, this doesn't look much like you, Wilbur,' said Winnie. 'Do you mind if it looks a bit, well, a bit, um, "modern"?'

'Mrrow!' said Wilbur when he saw it.

'That bad, eh?' said Winnie. Then she

had a look at the picture Wilbur had
just finished. It was a bit of a splatty cat
scribble. 'I don't look anything like that
. . . do I?' said Winnie. 'This painting
lark isn't as easy as it looks. Perhaps . . .'
Winnie reached for her wand.

'Meow!' Wilbur had a different idea.

He held up a paw to make Winnie stand
absolutely still. Then he put some paper
on the ground behind her. Next, he dipped
his tail into the pot of beetle-boot black
paint, and he carefully ran the end of his
tail all around the edge of Winnie's shadow
as it lay on the paper. From the tip of her
nose, along and up and round and down,
in and out and up and down until he got
back to her nose again to join up the line.

'Wow, Wilbur!' said Winnie. 'That is
one good-looking witch!'

Wilbur coloured it in.

134

'Well, we've got at least one good picture for the stairs,' said Winnie. 'Now it's my turn to do you.'

Wilbur posed, and Winnie painted around the outline of his shadow on the paper. Then she filled it in with black, all except for two big green eyes and blue triangle ears. Then she added a pink nose and some whiskers.

'Purrr!' said Wilbur when he saw it.

137

They called Jerry and Scruff over from next door.

'There's just time to do Jerry before we stop for lunch,' said Winnie. 'We'll need a whole roll of wallpaper to fit a giant on!'

But, strangely, Jerry's shadow picture came out shorter than Winnie expected.

'Ooer,' said Winnie. 'Jerry's not much bigger than you, Wilbur!'

'Is I?' said Jerry, scratching his head. 'Is I smaller than you, Winnie?'

'Yes!' said Winnie. 'You've shrunk yourself! It must be you doing the magic today Jerry because I haven't touched my wand!'

'So I is small *and* magical!' said Jerry with a giant grin.

As the afternoon went on, Mrs Parmar came to be painted, and some of the little ordinaries, and Winnie's three sisters. 'All my best people!' said Winnie. The strange thing was that Jerry's magic seemed to be working in the opposite direction as afternoon turned to evening. Some of the little ordinaries came out as giants. They liked that!

Mrs Parmar clapped her hands. 'You can tell your science teacher that you've learned all about how shadows are longer in the morning and evening and shorter in the middle of the day!' she said bossily, as she ushered the little ordinaries out of Winnie's garden.

So the truth was that Jerry hadn't actually shrunk himself at all! Which was just as well when it came to hanging the pictures up the side of Winnie's staircase. They needed a proper *giant* giant to do that!

'Brillaramaroodles!' said Winnie, as she looked at the pictures. 'That looks as perfect as a tarantula in a tutu! I shall smile when I go up the stairs now, even if the blooming power goes off again and we need to use wobbly candlelight!'

Winnie's Troublesome Wand

Winnie saw herself in the hall mirror, and sighed.

'Just look at that scraggy old hair! Maybe I should put it up today? In a bun? In a croissant? In a doughnut? What do you think, Wilbur?'

Wilbur yawned. Then—**plop!**—something was pushed through the letter flap, which immediately began munching it.

'Oi! Stop eating that, you naughty letter flap!' said Winnie, grabbing the envelope. She pulled out a card with fancy-nancy twiddly-twirly writing on it.

'A witchogram!' said Winnie. The card wiffled with nasty smells and seemed to bubble in her hand.

146

Luckily for Winnie, who wasn't at all good at reading, witchograms always read themselves out loud in witchy voices.

Winnie the Witch,
You are invited to come to
THE ANNUAL WITCHES' SPELLING
~ C O M P E T I T I O N ~
~ Held at ~
SCRATCHY BOTTOM HALL
this Friday 13th R.S.V.P.

INVITATIO

'Meow?' asked Wilbur, pointing at the RSVP.

'That means "reply soon (to be) very polite",' explained Winnie. 'I'll say "no". I don't like spelling tests.' So Winnie fed the card back to the letter flap. Then she felt in her cardigan pocket for her wand to send her reply witchogram. But her wand wasn't there. It wasn't in her dress pocket or her knickers pocket either. It wasn't *anywhere*.

'I had it just one maggoty minute ago!'
wailed Winnie. 'I can't do magic to find
the wand without having the wand to do
the magic to find that wand that I can't do
magic without. Oo, my head hurts!'

'Meow?' suggested Wilbur, pointing a
paw above his head.

'Of course!' said Winnie. 'Great Aunt Winifred's wand will be in her trunk in the attic. I'll use that one.'

Winnie and Wilbur went up the grand staircase —**clomp! clomp!**— up the spindly spiral stairs—**clankety clang!** —then up the wobbly rope ladder— **whoops!**—to push open the trap door— **creak!**—and climb up into the dark attic where things squeaked and scuttled.

There was a big musty fusty old trunk
in a corner.

'Great Auntie's trunk!' said Winnie.
She lifted up the lid—**creak!** Then
she plunged a hand into the trunk, and
brought out Great Aunt Winifred's . . .
best bloomers. **'Euch!'**

Winnie's fingers felt around in the trunk
some more and brought out . . .

'Great Auntie's wand!' said Winnie.
'Ooer, it does look a bit old-fashioned,
doesn't it. Do you think it still works?'

The wand *did* work, but in an old-
fashioned way. When Winnie wanted
better light to help her to climb down the
wobbly ladder she waved the old wand,

Abracadabra!

And instantly there were flickering
candle flames all over the attic.

'They'll set the house on fire!' said
Winnie. **Puff! Puff!** 'This whacky old
wand is just too old-fashioned, Wilbur.
I need a modern one.'

So Winnie went to her computer, and—**click! click!**—found Wendel's Wonderful World of Wands where she ordered the Silver Streak 13MXIII wand that had all the very latest features.

Ding dong! Ping pong! Sing a song!

'That's the doorbell,' said Winnie, hurrying downstairs. 'Witchmail is super fast!' She opened the door.

'Miss W. Watch?' asked the postman.

'It's *Witch*, not Watch!' said Winnie. 'Festering figs, do I look like a watch?'

'Well,' said the postman. 'You do have a face and two hands. Ha! Ha!'

'Do you want to be turned into a frog postman?' said Winnie.

'Er,' said the postman. 'No, Miss. Silly of me to say that. Could you please sign here, Miss Whatever-your-name-is?'

'Wow!' said Winnie as she drew the slender silver sparkling wand from the package. 'Look at all those buttons flashing, Wilbur!'

The first button Winnie tried made the wand invisible.

'Where's it gone?' said Winnie.

But then the wand let her know exactly where it was by poking her bottom. It reappeared, and made Winnie jump because it spoke.

What magic shall we perform MISTRESS?

'Oo,' said Winnie, licking her lips. 'I
would like a big squidgy chocolate puffball
filled with onion cream and sprinkled
with sugared ants.' She waved the wand.
'*Abracadabra!*'

But—**plonk!**—it wasn't a chocolate
puffball that instantly arrived.

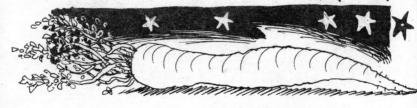

158

'That would not have been wise,'
explained the silver wand. 'I have replaced
your order with a healthier option. I hope
that you find it acceptable.'

'A carrot! I'm not a rotten rabbit,
you know!' said Winnie. 'Humph! I'm
going to magic my lovely old scruffy
wand back!' She waved the silver wand.
'Abracadabra!'

But the new wand knew better about that wish too.

'Oh no, Mistress,' it hissed. 'No, no, no. You mustn't replace me. Emphatically *no*.'

'But I don't want you!' Winnie threw the wand as far as she could but it just swerved around and came back to her.

She shoved the wand into a drawer and slammed it shut but the drawer slid back open, and the silver wand flew to Winnie again.

'Oh, you can't lose me, Mistress!' said the silvery wand. 'Oh, no, no!'

'Go away!' said Winnie.

'Hiss!' said Wilbur.

'Run for it!' said Winnie.

Winnie and Wilbur fled from the
house, slamming the door behind them.
Winnie stopped in the garden. 'What are
we going to do now?' wailed Winnie, and
she clutched at her head in despair. 'Oh, if
only I had my . . .' and suddenly Winnie
felt something thin and hard and long in
her hair, holding it all up. 'My old wand!'
Winnie pulled, and her hair tumbled.
'I didn't lose it after all!'

Just then—**crash!**—Winnie's door
flung itself open and the silver wand came
streaking towards them.

'Help!' said Winnie, holding her dear
old wand out as if it was a sword.

Soon she was—**crick! crack!**—
crossing wands with the silver wand.
Sparks flew, and splinters came off the dear
old wand. Then there was a deafening cry.
'Mrroww!' Wilbur ran from the house
with Great Aunt Winifred's wand. All
three wands battled together until—
crack!—one of them fell to the ground.
Winnie peeped between her fingers. The
silver wand had cracked in two. It wasn't
fizzing. It wasn't talking.

'Phewy!' said Winnie. 'I'm going to give that silver wand a new job to do. I do hope that it finds it acceptable!'

'Me-he-he!' laughed Wilbur as Winnie pinned her hair back up with a criss-cross of silver sticks.

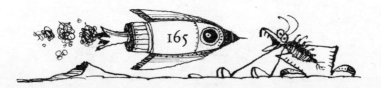

165

Spooky Winnie

One morning, at the end of October, Mrs Parmar came calling at Winnie's house.

'**Winniiee!**' yelled the dooryell.

'I have something for you,' said Mrs Parmar, putting an envelope into Winnie's hand. 'The children and I thought it might suit you.'

'What might suit me?' asked Winnie. But Mrs Parmar was already hurrying away.

'Meeow?' asked Wilbur.

'I've no idea at all,' said Winnie. 'Let's open it, and see.'

Winnie pulled out a card that read:

A Spiders, Spells and Spectres
SPECTACULAR
A HALLOWEEN PARTY
At the school tonight
Come in Spooky Fancy Dress
PLEASE
Bring decorations and food.

Winnie couldn't read all the words, but the children's pictures on the card helped her to understand.

168

'Whoopy doop, Wilbur! A Halloween party! We must get ready to go as soon as it gets dark tonight.'

'Let's make some decorations,' said Winnie. She whipped out her wand and waved it. *'Abracadabra!'*

169

Instantly there appeared a flock
of flapping black bats. They sorted
themselves into a line, held tiny bat
hands, and kicked their legs into a jig.
Bat bunting!

'Oh, they'll look lovely draped around
the school hall,' said Winnie. 'Especially
if they give a flutter and squeak every
now and again. I must bring some spiders

to make some spooky webs. We can
sprinkle the webs with glitter to look
pretty.' Winnie reached up to the top of
cupboards, and crouched down to look
under chairs, and ran her fingers along
floorboard cracks, picking up spiders.

'He he! They tickle!' she said. 'Now,
let's get Halloween cooking!'

Winnie and Wilbur looked at recipes, then they looked in the larder, and in the garden, and in the bin, and they collected ingredients. They chopped and chiselled and popped and topped and raked and baked. They made devilled gherkin ghastlies drizzled with real drizzle and dusted with real dust.

Slurp! Wilbur licked his lips.

WINNIIEE!

'They do look scrummy, don't they!' said
Winnie.

Outside it was getting dark. The moon
was shining. So were the stars.

'A perfect Halloween!' said Winnie.

'**Winniiee!**' yelled her dooryell again.

'Who ever can that be?' wondered Winnie.

173

'Oh, I should have said "what" ever instead of "who" ever!' said Winnie, because, there, on her doorstep, stood a little-ordinary devil and a little-ordinary ghoul.

'Trick or treat?' shouted the devil and the ghoul together, and they held out a pumpkin bucket that was already half full of sweets.

'I can choose, can I? Oh, goody goose pimples!' said Winnie. 'Hmm. Well, I think I'll do a trick then, thank you.' Winnie waved her wand then pointed it at the little-ordinary devil and the little-ordinary ghoul, and she shouted, *Abracadabra!'*

And, instantly, there were two little
toads, sitting on her doorstep. 'Will that
do?' asked Winnie.

'Croak! Croak!' said the ex-devil
and the ex-ghoul. Fat toady tears began to
fall down their warty green cheeks.

'Oh, dear!' said Winnie. 'Was that the
wrong sort of trick for you? Do you want
me to try something else?'

'Meow.' Wilbur whisper-explained to Winnie.

'Really?' said Winnie. 'Are you sure? *They* wanted to do a trick on *me*, did they? But wouldn't they like to stay as toads for the party?'

'Meeow!' Wilbur shook his head.

'All right, keep your fur on! I'll do it!' Winnie waved her wand again. '*Abracadabra!*'

Instantly the devil and the ghoul
reappeared, running away as fast as they
could.

'See?' said Winnie. 'They didn't want
to do anything to me after all. Now what
about my Halloween costume? It needs
to be spooky and it must go with having
a black cat, because you're coming to the
party too, Wilbur. Any ideas?'

Winnie got out her dressing-up box. 'I've been told that I'm batty,' she said, 'so how about a bat costume?'

The bat suit was far too small and far too tight. 'I'm squeezed as tight as toothpaste in a tube! This is no blooming good!'

179

So Winnie and Wilbur threw on a couple
of sheets, and tried being ghosts.

Trip-bang! 'I can't see where I'm
going,' said Winnie, 'and I can't see to take
food from a plate. Being a ghost is no good
at all!' They threw off their sheets.

'Oh, if only there was something spooky
that really suited a lady and a black cat!'

'Meow?' suggested Wilbur, holding up a

loo roll.

'The Egyptian-mummy look.' said
Winnie. 'Great! Wrap me up, Wilbur!'

Wilbur wound loo roll round and round
Winnie.

'Ooo, Wilbur!' said Winnie, her voice
muffled by loo paper. 'I can't move!'

So Wilbur pulled off the loo roll,

making Winnie spin like a top. 'Oh dear, I don't know what else I can try!' said dizzy Winnie.

'**Winniiee!**' yelled her dooryell *again*.

This time a little-ordinary skeleton and a little-ordinary ghost stood on the doorstep.

WINNIIEE!

'Boo!' said the little ghost.

'Boo who?' said Winnie.

'Don't cry!' said the little ghost.

'Oh, very funny!' said Winnie. 'Are you going to the party? Can we come with you?'

So Winnie and Wilbur went to the party dressed as plain old Winnie and plain old Wilbur, taking their food and decorations with them.

'Come in, come in!' said Mrs Pumpkin
Parmar when they got to the school.
'Come and join in the fun.'

There was apple bobbing.

And pin the cat on the broomstick.

'Mrrrow!' said Wilbur.

There was dancing to the Bony Band of
Skeletons.

'Don't stand still, Mrs Parmar!' said
Winnie. 'My spiders are making webs
on anything that stays still for a single
maggoty-moment! Dance to keep them off
you!'

So even Mrs Parmar joined in with the
dancing. Winnie and Wilbur went wild.

It was a hauntingly-horribly-happy Halloween party. And it ended with prizes for the best costumes, awarded by the headmaster. There were prizes for the best pumpkin, the best ghost, the best ghoul, the best skeleton, and the best witch.

'Your costume was quite a good effort,' the headmaster told Winnie. 'But not as good as this little witch, I'm afraid.' And he gave the prize to a little-ordinary witch.

'Humph!' said Winnie.

But then she found that her gherkin
ghastlies hadn't all been eaten at the party.
So she and Wilbur went home happily
chomping ghastlies and spotting spooks as
they walked home through the Halloween
night.

Detective Winnie

'Ooo, Wilbur!' Winnie clutched poor Wilbur as if he was a cushion. She peeped around him at the television. 'That poor lady has been kidnapped! She's been tied like a sweet flea plant to a stake, and she can't escape! Ooo, whatever is going to happen to her?'

'**Mrrugug!**' gurgled poor Wilbur.

On the television, Detective Derek had found Bad Boris in his woodland den.

'Where have you hidden her, Boris? That handbag doesn't go with your outfit, so I know it isn't yours. It must be stolen. It's hers, isn't it! But what have you done with her, eh?'

'Shan't tell!' said Bad Boris.

'Oh poor lady!' said Winnie.

But cunning Detective Derek was already solving the crime.

'Those are strange footprints, Bad Boris,' he said. 'Your left footprints are blue while your right ones are yellow. So I reckon you've got her in that old paint factory!'

'It's true, I have!' wailed Bad Boris.

So the lady was rescued from the paint factory, and given back her handbag. Winnie turned off the televison.

'He's as clever as a clog, that Detective Derek!' said Winnie.

The next morning Winnie and Wilbur were in the village when…

'Yap yap yap!'

'Whatever's that?' said Winnie. 'Oo, look, Wilbur! There's a dear little doggy tied up to that post, just like the lady on the telly. He must have been dognapped by a baddie like Bad Boris!'

'Meeo!' Wilbur was shaking his head.

YAP YAP
YAP YAP
YAP
YAP
YAP

'We must save him!' said Winnie.

'That's what Detective Derek would do!'

So Winnie untied the little dog, and popped it into her shopping bag. Then they went home. **Yarooo! Yap yap yap!** noises came from the bag.

'He's just upset by being dognapped,' said Winnie.

193

Back home, Winnie took the dog from the bag.

'Grrr snap!'

'You're not a crocodile, so stop that!' said Winnie, snatching her fingers out of the dog's way. 'You're frightened, aren't you, you poor little pooch?'

Winnie offered the dog a bowl of bat's milk.

'Grrr!'

'Would a big brave kind of a name help you?' said Winnie. 'I'm going to call you Butch.'

'Grrr!' said Butch. **'Yap yap yap!'**

Winnie covered her ears. 'We'd better get detecting, and find out where Butch really belongs. Then we can give him back to his grateful owner. Get thinking like a detective, Wilbur! Baddies like Boris live in woodland lairs so that's where we'll go.

Winnie grabbed everything they might need for detective work: a magnifying glass, a torch, a scribble-book, and some jam jars for samples.

'**Yap yap yap!**' said Butch as Winnie
and Wilbur shut him in the house. They
got on to the broom.

'We must go to the woods!' said Winnie,
and off they flew until they landed with a
bump in the middle of a clump of trees.

'Can you see any bad burglar types?'
Winnie asked Wilbur. **Squelch!** One of
Winnie's shoes had fallen off. **Hop-bop
hop-bop.** She used her broom as a
crutch as she hopped to a log and put the
shoe back on.

198

They made their way through the wood,
peering and listening and sniffing for clues
but they only found twigs and leaves and
rabbit poos. Soon they were back in the
village. And there they did find a clue!

'A footprint!' said Winnie. 'That's
just the sort of clue we need! Oo, there's
another one! Very suspicious! I reckon
they must belong to a burglar!'

Winnie took a deep breath. 'We've got
to be as brave as a chicken asking a fox for
a dance now, Wilbur. Come on!'

The suspicious footprints led Winnie
and Wilbur straight back to the wood.

'I *knew* we'd find our burglar in the
wood,' said Winnie. But then, 'Ooer,
that's strange,' said Winnie. 'There's only
a left footprint here. A left footprint, then
another left footprint, then a little round
thing instead of a right footprint. Oo, I
know what that means!'

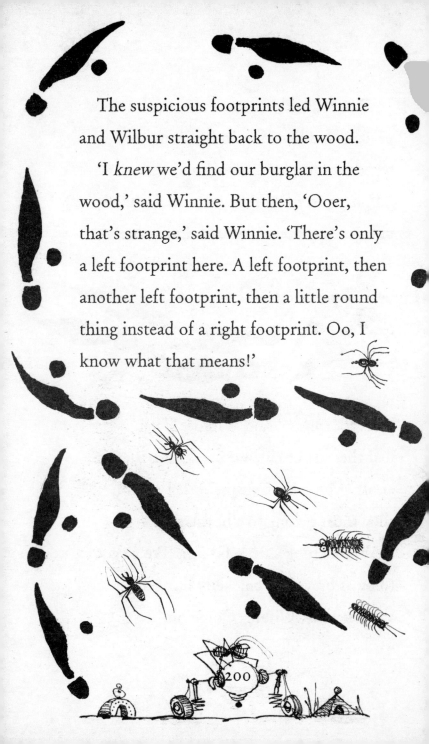

200

'Meow?' said Wilbur.

'It means that our dog-napper is someone with a wooden leg. A pirate!'

Then the footprints with the wooden-leg prints stopped. 'So where is the pilfering pirate?' said Winnie. They couldn't find him in the wood, and there were no other clues to follow, so they flew home.

A lot of howling was coming from
Winnie's house.

'Poor little Butchy,' said Winnie. Then
she noticed the suspicious footprints
outside her house.

'Oh, no!' she screeched, 'the pirate must
be inside my house!' Winnie picked up
Wilbur and clutched him like a cushion
again. 'No wonder little Butchy is howling!'

Wilbur jumped down and pointed to
where Winnie had just taken a step . . .
leaving a suspicious footprint from
her shoe.

MEOW!

'Oo, Wilbur!' said Winnie. 'You don't think ... ?'

'Meow!' nodded Wilbur.

'So we've been tracking *me* all along?' said Winnie. 'I am the pirate?' Gulp! went Winnie. 'I never knew I was a pirate! So, oh golly-mollykins, I didn't rescue Butch, at all. I dog-napped him! Oo, Wilbur, maybe his owner was inside the shop all along? Er, do you think we can sneak Butch back before anybody notices?'

They popped Butch back into Winnie's bag, and they flew back to the shop. Winnie was just tying Butch back to the lamp post when Winnie's sister Wilma burst out of the shop.

'Oh, Winnie, you've *found* my little
darling!' said Wilma, pouncing on Butch.

'I didn't mean to dog-nap him . . .'
began Winnie. Then she realized what
Wilma had said. 'Er, that's right, Wilma,'
said Winnie. 'I found Butch. That's what
I did. Is he yours, Wilma?'

'She's a *she*, not a *he*!' said Wilma. 'She's called Fluffball.'

'Fluffball!' said Winnie.

'Me-he-he!' said Wilbur.

'**Grrr! Yap!**' said Fluffball-Butch.

'I think she's saying "thank you, Auntie Winnie",' cooed Wilma.

'Mmm,' said Winnie and she left, rather quickly.

'I don't speak Dog,' said Winnie
when they got home, 'but I think that
Fluffball was saying something as rude as
a barnacle's bottom to us back there, and
not "thank you" at all!'

'Meow?' said Wilbur.

208

'I do understand Cat, though,' said
Winnie. 'Yes, let's have that nice cup of
stink-weed tea and an evil-weevil biscuit.
We're just in time for the next Detective
Derek Mystery on the telly.'

Winnie's Different Day

Winnie's alarm croc snapped its teeth.

Snip-snap, snip-snap!

'Get up Winniiee. Get up, Wilburr!' it snapped, just as it did every day.

'All right, half left!' grumbled Winnie. 'I'm getting out of bed, aren't I?' Winnie tipped out of her bed on the right side, just as she always did. She shoved her feet into her slip-sloppers, first the left one then the right one, just as she always did.

She went to the bathroom and she was just washing her face in the same sort of way as she always did when a thought hit her like a slap round the cheeks with a wet fish.

'You know what, Wilbur?' said Winnie, splashing her hands into the soapy water in the sink. 'I'm bored with doing the same ordinary things in the same ordinary-as-a-centipede-running-out-of-socks way, day after day after day.'

Wilbur licked his right paw and stroked it over his head, then lifted his left leg to have a wash under that.

'And you're just as boring as I am! You always do that while I'm washing my face!' Wilbur stopped still, leg in the air, tongue hanging out.

213

'Go on. Finish doing it,' said Winnie.
'You enjoy tasting all those fur flavours.
And I've got to wash my face otherwise
there will be sleepy bits in my eyes all day
long.'

Winnie spoke to her back-to-front
self in the mirror. 'We do have to do the
ordinary things, but we don't have to do
them in ordinary ways, do we? Let's have a
Doing Things Differently Day today!'

So Winnie put her dress on back to front. That felt new and interesting. She combed all the tangles out of her hair and plaited it neatly. It did look *very* different. She walked backwards instead of forwards down the stairs—**bump! crash!** She ate her breakfast porridge with a fork instead of a spoon, and she put pepper and mustard on it instead of sweet-bug syrup.

'Very nice!' said Winnie.

Then she hopped upstairs and brushed her teeth, holding the brush in her right hand instead of her left and starting from the opposite side to normal.

She got ready to go out. 'We do need to get a few bits and blobs of shopping, Wilbur. Fetch the bags, will you, and I'll get my broom and purse.'

217

Winnie and Wilbur sat backwards on
the broom to be different. It was a rather
uncomfortable way to be different. When
they got to the shop, Winnie gave the
shopkeeper her list.

'Biscuits, bread, bin liners, bunion
cream,' he read, in a boringly ordinary
voice.

'What a boringly ordinary list!' said
Winnie. Then Winnie noticed some little
ordinaries who didn't seem to be finding
their shopping ordinary or boring at all.

'One of those!'

'A bag of them!'

'What sort of shopping are you doing?'
Winnie asked them.

'We've each got thirteen pence pocket money to spend,' explained one little ordinary. 'We're choosing which sweets to buy. There are jelly snakes, fizzy dabs, scrunch munch pellets, biteable bead bangles, gob stoppers, milk bottles, liquorice laces, sherbet bombs, chewy strawberries, chocolate bars, trillions and billions . . .'

'Ooh, pocket money sounds fun to
spend.' Winnie opened her toad purse.
'I've only got boring ordinary money
in my purse. Where do you get pocket
money from?'

'We earn it by doing little jobs,' the
little ordinaries told her.

So Winnie and Wilbur went off to do
some little jobs.

Winnie tried busking. But she was so out of tune that no-one gave her any money.

Then Winnie tried cleaning windscreens. But she forgot to ask people to close their windows before she threw her bucket of water.

'You'll have to pay me for the damage!' said a cross, soggy driver.

Then Winnie set up a stall selling hop-corn flop-corn plop-corn rot-corn not-corn, but nobody bought any at all.

Wilbur did some little jobs, too.

He caught mice, he warmed knees, he polished anything that needed polishing.

'I haven't earned anything!' sighed Winnie.

Wonderful Winnie

223

'Meeow!' Wilbur proudly held out his coins.

'Yippee!' Winnie danced a little dance. 'Clever you, Wilbur! Now we've got lots of pocket money!'

'Meow!' Wilbur turned Winnie around
to make her look away from him, then he
hid coins here and there and everywhere
and turned Winnie back to look.

'Where have all the coins gone?' said
Winnie. 'Ooh, I see! It's a pocket-money
treasure hunt!' And off she scampered,
peering and pouncing and picking up coins.

The little ordinaries joined the treasure hunt and they all found coins, too. Then they all went pocket-money shopping together.

227

'Oh, this is much more fun than ordinary shopping!' said Winnie. 'I'll have three humming bugs, and one rubble gum, and one big gob slobber, please. Oh, and a fizzy fish and two mint mice for Wilbur.'

Winnie and Wilbur walked home,
scoffing sweets.

'Different is good!' sighed Winnie—

chew! scrunch! munch! 'And sweets
are nice. But now I fancy something fresh
and juicy. Can you guess what I'm going
to do with my last pocket-money penny,
Wilbur?'

'Meow?' Wilbur shook his head.

'I'm going to throw it into that wishing
well!' **Plop!** went the penny. Then Winnie
closed her eyes and wished as hard as she
could.

'Meow?' said Wilbur, pointing at
Winnie's wand.

'Oh I know,' said Winnie, opening one
eye. 'But I can do *that* sort of magic any old
day, and I'm doing things differently today,
remember? Now, let me wish my wish.'

And suddenly—**splat-splat-splat!**—it was raining pong berries, just as Winnie had wished for! She held out her shopping bag to catch them.

'Well, that *was* a different sort of shopping!' laughed Winnie, stuffing purple pong berries into her mouth.

'When we get home, Wilbur, I'm going to sleep upside down in my bed, to be different. Then tomorrow we'll go back to being ordinary. But all the ordinary things will feel nice and different because we've had a holiday from them. That's a kind of magic!'

Woolly Wilbur

Winnie woke-up with a blue nose with icicle drips on the end of it. Her teeth were clacking like tap-dancing skeletons. The only bit of her that was warm was her tummy, and that was because fat furry Wilbur was curled up, purring on top of it.

'It's s-s-so c-c-cold!' said Winnie. 'We'd b-b-better g-g-get up, Wilbur. L-l-light the f-f-fire to w-w-warm the house.'

Winnie got dressed fast, then she and Wilbur hurried downstairs. Drifty-draughty cold winds whistled under Winnie's doors and around Winnie's windows and up her skirt.

'I need a n-n-nice big m-m-mug of c-c-cocoa!' said Winnie, licking her lips at the thought of that sweet, smooth, chocolaty taste running down through her body pipes like a radiator system to warm her from the inside.

'M-m-meow!' agreed Wilbur. He pulled
open the fridge door, but, 'Mrrrow!'

'No milk?' said Winnie. 'Oh, bats'
bottoms, that means no hot chocolate!
And I so fancy a drink of hot chocolate!
We'll just have to go and buy some milk.'

Winnie opened the front door.

'Look, it's snowing!' said Winnie. 'Where in this w-w-white world are our w-w-woollies, Wilbur?'

Wilbur pulled open the door of the cupboard under the stairs, and out flew four fat happily chomping moths.

'Those mean moths have munched our mittens to bits!' wailed Winnie. 'They've hogged our hats and snacked on our scarves! Oh, Wilbur, we can't go out in this snowy cold without woollies to keep us warm. We'd freeze as solid as frog fingers fresh from the freezer!'

'Meow?' suggested Wilbur, doing some strange movements with his paws.

'Good idea!' said Winnie. 'We just need to find some wool, and then I'll knit-knot some lovely new warm winter woollies for us to wear!'

But when they opened the wool cupboard, out flew five even fatter moths!

'You greedy, gobbling, fluttering, stealing, miserable moths!' Winnie was jumping up and down with rage, trying to whack the moths, but they flittered away and she only whacked the ornaments and poor Wilbur. 'How on earth are we going to get wool to knit some woollies to keep us warm enough to go out into the snow to walk to the shop to buy some milk to make hot chocolate, eh?'

Wilbur shrugged, but Winnie's face was suddenly stretching into a big smile. She pulled her wand from her pocket. 'Of course!' she said. 'What we need is sheep! A flock of fat fluffy sheep!' Winnie waved her wand. *Abracadabra!*

For a moment or two it seemed as if no magic had happened. But when Winnie opened the front door to check if there were any sheep on the doorstep, Wilbur pointed to the sky. A flurry of snow was falling, falling, falling in that way that makes you feel dizzy.

'Waddling wombats!' said Winnie. 'I've never seen such big snowflakes!'

Then Wilbur jumped out of the way
just in time as—**thump!**—a sheep landed
where he had been standing. **Thump!**
Thump! More and more sheep landed in
the snow by the doorway, and then they
baa-rged their way into the house.

244

'Well,' said Winnie. 'I ordered a flock of sheep, so they've flown down like a flock of birds! Shut the door, Wilbur, and let's get shearing!'

It was quite fun clipping the sheep into interesting shapes. Not as much fun for the sheep, of course. Wilbur made his sheep look odd. Winnie made her sheep look very, very odd.

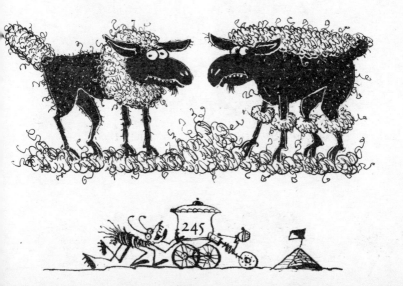

But they soon had a pile of what looked like dirty candy floss.

'It's got to be spun into balls of wool before we can knit with it,' said Winnie. 'Spindly-spiders are the best spinners.' Winnie waved her wand. *Abracadabra!*

Instantly there were spiders, with lots of legs wriggle-spinning the fluffy wool.

246

'Hold out your arms, Wilbur!' said
Winnie. 'Now we need to wind the wool.'

Then, at last, they were ready to start
knitting.

'Well,' said Winnie. 'All that work
has warmed me up a bit, but it's made
me thirsty too. I really, really want a big
bubbling mug of hot chocolate more than
ever now, so let's knit really, really fast!'

247

Winnie tried knitting with broom handles. 'The fatter the needles are, the faster the knitting grows,' she said. 'I'm making you a tail warmer, Wilbur!' **Knit knit, clickety-click!**

But Winnie's knitting was just too big! 'This is no good, it's like a flipping fisherman's net!' said Winnie. 'You can't wear this, Wilbur!'

'I'll try knitting with wands instead,'
said Winnie. **Knit knit, clickety-
click!** 'Ah, that's much better!'

Winnie knitted hats and gloves and
tail warmers and scarves and ponchos.

'Meow!' said Wilbur, pointing to the clock.

'That's true,' said Winnie. 'We'd better go and get that milk before the shops shut.'

So they put on all their new woollies, and they opened the front door, and ... didn't go anywhere because there was a white wall of snow completely filling the doorway. 'We're trapped!' wailed Winnie. 'Oh no! And I do so want a drink of hot chocolate!'

Wilbur dug the snow. Winnie shovelled
the snow. But they couldn't shovel a path
all the way into the village in time before
the shops shut.

251

'I know what we can do,' said Winnie.
She took off her tights (she had two pairs
on!). Then she tied them to her knitted
netting and fixed everything to the gate
posts. 'There!' she said.

'Meow?' asked Wilbur.

'It's a catapult!' said Winnie. 'A catapult
to hurl you all the way to the shops to get
some milk!'

252

'Mrrooww!' protested Wilbur, but Winnie was already loading him, along with a bag and purse, into the catapult.

Tug tug twang!

Neeeoow! Wilbur shot over the snow to land—**flump!**—just outside the shop.

'Yay, that looks fun!' said the little ordinaries. 'How did you do that, Wilbur?'

253

The little ordinaries waited for Wilbur
to get the milk, then they dug him a path
back to Winnie's house so that they could
all take it in turns to be catapulted—
flump!—into the snow. And Winnie
brewed a whole cauldron of hot chocolate
for everyone to share.

'With lovely toasted-ant hundreds
and thousands sprinkles and mushroom-
mallows!' said Winnie.

The little ordinaries were so very
grateful for the goes on the catapult that
they said that Winnie should have all
the sprinkles and mushroom-mallows
on her cup, and they didn't take any for
themselves. 'Aren't they such nice-as-lice
little ordinaries?' said Winnie, resting her
feet up on a nice warm sheep.

255

Winnie Goes Wild!

'Winnie, are you listening to me?'
screeched Winnie's sister Wendy down
the telling moan. 'I don't want you
embarrassing me in front of my friends.
It's a barbecue with an exotic theme so
you've got to look *exotic!* OK?'

'I haven't got anything exotic to wear,'
said Winnie, who wasn't at all in the mood
for one of Wendy's parties.

'See you at six,' nagged Wendy. **Click!**

And that was the end of the moan call.

'**Mnfff,**' said Winnie from under
the frantically frilly party frock she was
struggling to put on.

'Meow?' asked Wilbur as he watched
Winnie wriggling into her dress.

'I said that I think it's going to rain and
make the sausages squelchy at Wendy's
barbecue,' huffed Winnie, popping her
head through the party frock neck. She

pulled the dress down, and looked at
herself in the mirror. 'Not very exotic, is it?'
Winnie waved her wand. *Abracadabra!*

And instantly, there on her head, was a
hat made of pineapple and bananas and
grapes. It wobbled, but the grapes were tasty.

'Yum!' said Winnie, popping a grape into her mouth. 'We'd better get going, Wilbur, before I eat all my hat.'

They climbed aboard Winnie's broom, and took off, up into the cloudy sky.

'Ooer!' said Winnie as the broom swerved this way and that in the wiffly-waffly wind. Wilbur closed his eyes and held on tight. The wind whipped Winnie's hat ribbons undone and tossed the fruit from her head. 'Oh, no!' wailed Winnie as rain began to splatter. Soon Wilbur was a soggy cat, and Winnie was a drippy witch. Then it began to hail. **Ping ping!** Cold hard pellets pelted them.

'Ow! Ow!' said Winnie.

'Me-Ow! Me-Ow!' said Wilbur.

But just then the wind suddenly blew
them into a big billowing blue-black cloud
that rumbled thunder around them and
bumped them about.

'Wilburrr!' shouted Winnie as she fell
off her broom . . . down through the soft
wet cloud.

'Grab hold of my hand, Wilbur!'
shouted Winnie, and, paw-in-hand, they
fell together down through the cloud.
Then down through the trees, which
ripped and snagged their clothes as they
fell, until finally they landed with a bump
on the ground.

'Where in the whoopsy-world are we?'
wondered Winnie.

'Hiss!'

263

'It's no good hissing about it, Wilbur,' began Winnie. But then, 'Oh,' she said. It wasn't Wilbur who was hissing. **Clack clack clack!** Wilbur's knees knocked together because a huge snake was slithering past them!

Chit chat! went a monkey.

Squawk! went a bright birdie.

Steam! went the air all around.

'Uh-oh,' said Winnie. 'I think we've
landed in a jungle! What are we going to
do about Wendy's party? She's going to be
a crotchety-cross witch if we're late! Or
if we're not looking right.' Winnie looked
at Wilbur. 'Oh, dear, you are one mega-
messy moggy. You look as if you've been
dragged through a tree backwards. I can't
take you to Wendy's looking like that! You
need a wash!'

'Mrrow!' protested Wilbur, as
Winnie picked him up and dangled
him over a marshy pool of green water.
Then, **'Urgh!'** said Winnie. There was
something hideously horrible in the water!
'Whatever can that be?'

The horrible thing in the water
wobbled, talking silently as Winnie talked
out loud. 'Oh, no!' screeched Winnie. The
horrible thing was her own reflection!

'I look worse than you do, Wilbur!' said Winnie.

But, just then, the reflected Winnie wobbled and—**snap!**—up came the jaws of an alligator! The alligator fancied Wilbur's furry worm of a tail for his tea!

Winnie whipped out her wand, and waved it, '*Abracadabra!*' And instantly the last ribbon holding up what was left of her ragged party dress whirled from her waist, and it tied the alligator's jaws tight in a big pink bow.

'**Sngrr!**' went the alligator.

'The ribbon won't hold for long!' warned Winnie. 'Run for it!'

Winnie scrabbled up a tree. Very soon she was surrounded by monkeys. They were poking and scratching and **ooh-ooh-ooh-ing.**

'Wilbur!' said Winnie. 'Where are you?'

Then Winnie saw Wilbur. He was padding along the branch towards her.

'Ooh, Wilbur, you do look smart!' said Winnie. 'How did you tidy yourself up so quickly?'

'**Purrr!**' went Wilbur as he padded
closer. His purr was louder and lower than
usual. The branch bent under the weight
of his sleek black body.

'Er, Wilbur?' said Winnie. 'Um, what
big paws you've got, Wilbur. What
big eyes you've got, Wilbur. Oh, no!

270

Oh, help!' shouted Winnie because she suddenly realized that this Wilbur wasn't Wilbur after all! This was a panther, and it was opening its toothy greedy grin as it got ready to pounce on her . . .

Just as—'Mrrow!'—real, dear Wilbur was swinging through the trees with a troop of monkeys who snatched Winnie to safety.

It was rather nice being swung through the trees, nearly naked. Winnie and Wilbur collected things as they went. **Whoops!** —some leaves— **whoops!**—some feathers—**whoops!**—some nuts and flowers and fruits and vines and jungle bugs.

By the time they came down to land, Winnie's and Wilbur's legs were like jelly, but they had collected enough things to make an exotic outfit for Winnie, with just one wave of her wand. *Abradcadabra!* All ready for Wendy's party,' said Winnie.

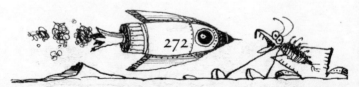

The monkeys brought them their broom, and soon they were flying up and out of the jungle.

274

The stormy weather had cleared, and they landed in Wendy's garden just as Wendy was checking her watch.

'We're here!' shouted Winnie. 'And we've brought you some exotic fruits and exotic nuts for your exotic party.' Winnie handed over their plate of jungle goodies. Then she collapsed into a deckchair, with a happy sigh.

'But . . .' said Wendy, her eyes popping and her mouth dropping open in surprise. 'You look exceptionally, extremely, extraordinarily exotic! You told me that you hadn't got anything exotic to wear, Winnie! So where did you get your outfit?'

'Oh, we went a bit wild and picked these things up in a jungle-sale,' said Winnie. *Abracadabra!* Winnie casually waved her wand, and her broom instantly burst into exotic flowers.

'Now, that's just showing off!' said Wendy.

And Finally . . .

Why did Winnie give up tap dancing?

She kept falling into the sink.

What do you call Winnie's sister
Wilma who lives by the sea?

A sandwitch.

Did you hear about the witch
who tried to iron her curtains?

She fell out of the window.

Why does a witch ride on a broom?

Because a vacuum cleaner is too noisy.

How does a witch tell the time?

She wears a witch watch.

Who turns the lights off at Halloween?

The lights witch.

Why couldn't the witch talk on the phone?

She had a frog in her throat.

How can you tell that fish are musical?

Send for the piano tuna.

Which fish terrorizes other fish?

Jack the Kipper.

What's the best way to communicate with a fish?

Drop it a line.

What lies at the bottom of the sea and is very dangerous?

Billy the Squid.

What do you call a man with an elephant on his head?

Squashed.

What's the difference between an African elephant and an Indian elephant?

About 3000 miles.

What's the difference between an elephant and a biscuit?

You can't dip an elephant in your tea.

What do you call an elephant that flies?

A jumbo jet.

What should you do if you find
a dinosaur in your bed?

Sleep somewhere else.

How do you ask a dinosaur to dinner?

Tea, Rex?

Why did the dinosaur cross the road?

Chickens hadn't been invented yet.

What do you get when dinosaurs
crash their cars?

Tyrannosaurus wrecks.

What do computers have for lunch?

Spam and chips.

There's a spider in Winnie's computer.

What's he doing?

He's set up his own website.

Why does Dracula like computers?

Because they've got so many bytes in them.

Why did the footballer kick his computer?

He wanted to boot up the system.

Wilbur

Winnie the Witch

The Head Teacher

The Little Ordinaries

Wilma

Mrs Parmar

Enjoy more magic moments
with Winnie the Witch!

www.winnie-the-witch.com